Webster

written by
Martin Waddell

For Emily, Daniel and Katie—M.W.

For Danny—D.P.

First published 2001 by Walker Books Ltd, 87 Vauxhall Walk, London SE11 5HJ

10 9 8 7 6 5 4 3 2   Text © 2001 Martin Waddell   Illustrations © 2001 David Parkins

The right of Martin Waddell to be identified as author of this work has been asserted
by him in accordance with the Copyright, Designs and Patents Act 1988

This book has been typeset in ITC Tiffany   Printed in Hong Kong

British Library Cataloguing in Publication Data:
a catalogue record for this book is available from the British Library

ISBN 0-7445-7527-3

J. Duck

illustrated by
David Parkins

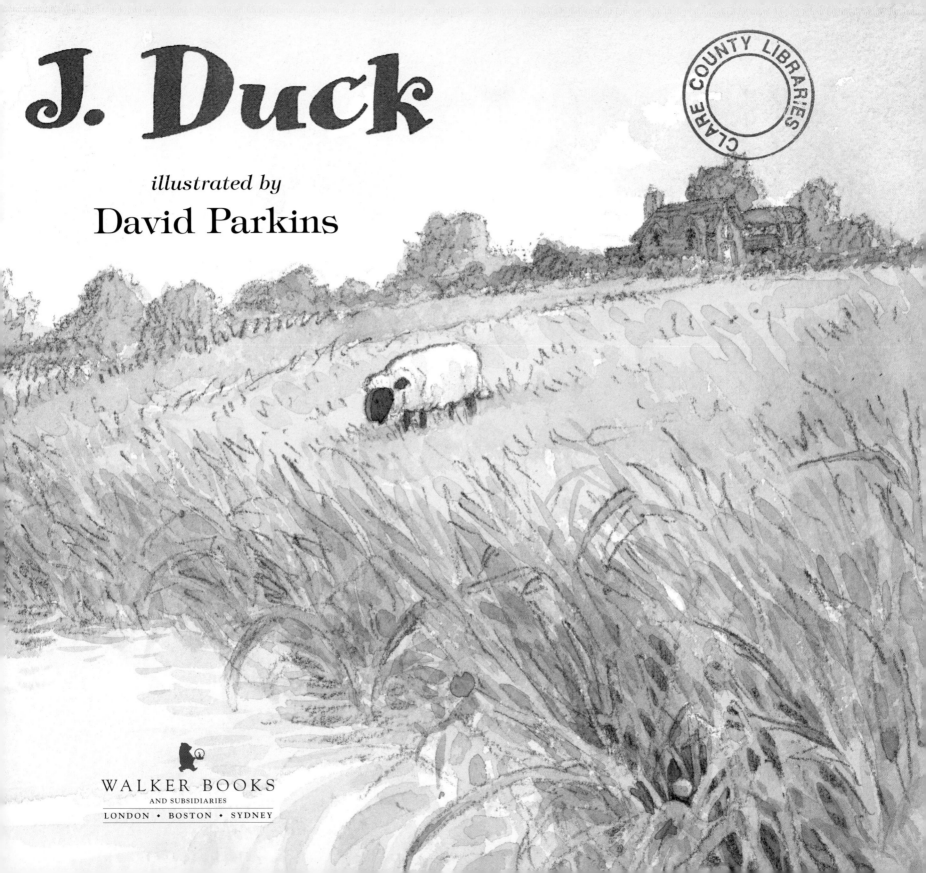

WALKER BOOKS
AND SUBSIDIARIES
LONDON · BOSTON · SYDNEY

There was once

a duck egg hidden away in the
reeds by the bank of the lake.
In the duck egg was wee
Webster J. Duck all folded up
so he'd fit in the egg.

Webster stirred
in the egg.

He tapped the eggshell
with his beak and ...

C-R-A-C-K!
The shell broke.

Out of the egg came
wee Webster J. Duck.

Webster J. Duck stood on the
bits of shell he had broken.
"Where is my mum?" Webster thought.
"I must have a mum,
because all baby ducks do."

Webster went

"Quack-
quack,
quack-
quack!"

calling his mum,

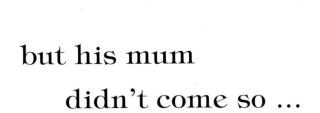

but his mum
didn't come so ...

Webster J. Duck set off to find her.

Webster met a Duck with a Waggledy Tail,
down by the side of the lake.

"Quack-quack?"
asked Webster J. Duck.

"Bow-wow!"

went the Duck with the Waggledy Tail.

"You're not my mum," Webster thought.
"My mum would go quack-quack
like me!"

Then Webster met a Bigger Big Duck, with big ears and an udder.

"Quack-quack?" asked Webster J. Duck.

"Moo-moo!" went the Bigger Big Duck.

"You're not my mum," Webster thought. "My mum would go quack-quack like me!"

Webster J. Duck sat down and cried
by the edge of the lake.
His little duck feathers were shiny
with tiny duck tears.

"Quack, quack, quack,"
sobbed Webster.

"**BOW-WOW!**"
barked the Duck with
the Waggledy Tail.

"**BAA-BAA!**"
baa-ed the Big
Woolly Duck.

"MOO-MOO-MOO-MOO!"

moo-ed the Bigger Big Duck.

They were trying to help by

calling his mum ...

but the BOW-WOWs and
the BAAs and the MOOs
scared Webster J. Duck.
He hid his little duck
head under his wing,
and he quivered
and shivered and
shook and he went
"Quack-quack,"
all alone.

And then someone answered
"QUACK-QUACK!"
(just like Webster's quack, but
quite a bit louder).

QUACK-QUACK! QUACK-

Mum Duck came through
the reeds.

And Webster swam off
with his mum.

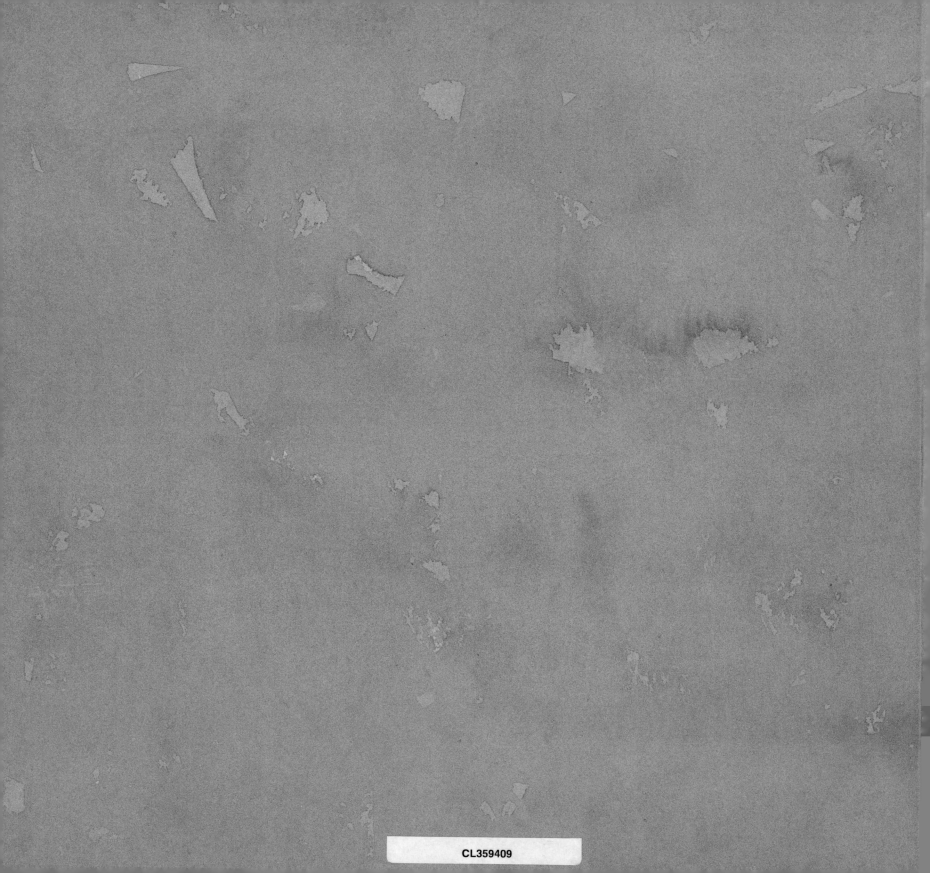